Words by
Jordan Scott

Pictures by
Sydney Smith

I TALK LIKE A RIVER

NEAL PORTER BOOKS
HOLIDAY HOUSE/NEW YORK

I wake up

with the sounds of words

each morning

all around me.

P for the pine tree outside my bedroom window.

C for the crow in its branches.

M for the moon fading in the morning sky.

I wake up each morning with the sounds of words all around me.

And I can't say them all.

The P
  in pine tree
    grows roots
  inside my mouth
and tangles
  my tongue.

The C is a crow
  that sticks
    in the back
  of my throat.

The M in moon
  dusts my lips
    with a magic
    that makes me
  only mumble.

I wake up in the
morning with these
word-sounds stuck
in my mouth.

I stay quiet
as a stone.

I eat my oatmeal without a peep.
I get ready for the day without a word.

At school, I hide in the back of class.
I hope I don't have to talk.

When my teacher asks me a question,
all my classmates turn and look.

They don't see
    a pine tree sticking
      out from my lips
instead of
    a tongue.

They don't hear
    a crow *Caw! Caw!*
    from inside
      my throat.

They don't hide
    their eyes from
      the moonlight
    that shines from
my open mouth.

All they hear is how I don't talk like them.
All they see is how strange my face looks
and that I can't hide how scared I am.

My mouth isn't working.
It's full with words
of the morning.

Mornings are always
hard, but this one's
especially tough.
I'm more stuck
than ever.

My teacher says
we all have to talk
about our
favorite place
in the world.

Today is my turn
but my mouth
just isn't working,
and I want to go home.

My dad picks me up from school.
"It's just a bad speech day," he says.
"Let's go somewhere quiet."

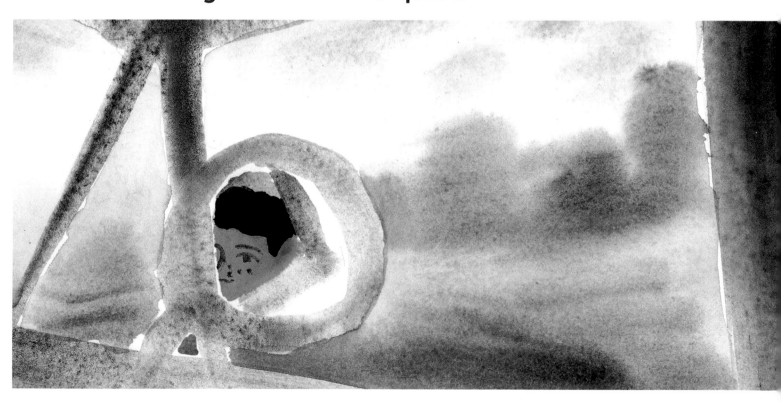

My dad takes me to the river.

We walk along the shore looking for colorful rocks and water bugs.

It feels good to be quiet
and alone with my dad.

But I can't stop thinking
about my bad speech day:

All those eyes watching
    my lips
        twist and twirl,

all those mouths
        giggling
        and laughing.

I feel a storm in my belly;
my eyes fill with rain.

My dad sees I am sad and pulls me
close; he points to the river and says:

"See how that water moves?
That's how you speak."

I look at the water

bubbling,

whirling,

churning,

and crashing.

My dad says I talk like a river.

This is what I like to remember,
to help stop myself from crying

I talk like a river

or from not wanting to speak at all.

I talk like a river

When the words around me are hard to say, I think of the proud river,

bubbling,

churning,

whirling,

and crashing.

And I also think of the calm river beyond the rapids where the water is smooth and glistening.

This is how my mouth moves.

This is how I speak.

Even the river stutters.

Like I do.

I wake up in the morning
  with the sounds of words
all around me.

I go to school and tell the class about
my favorite place in the world.

I talk about the river.

And I talk like a river.

How I Speak

When I was a boy my dad would sometimes pick me up from school on "bad speech days" and take me down to the river. On those days my mouth would just stop working. Every word was painful; the laughter from classmates unbearable. I just wanted to be quiet. Along the river we skipped stones, watched for salmon, picked up bugs, and plucked blackberries, all without saying a word.

One particular day, while watching the water move against the shore, my dad said: "You see how that water moves, son? That's how you speak."

Stuttering is often mocked because it is seen as unnatural. For many, listening to and watching someone stutter is not a comfortable experience because language and sound are stretched to their limits. Strange noises burst from a contorting mouth, and what the listener thinks of as fluency or "normal speech" explodes. To stutter is to be dysfluent; and fluency, my speech therapist used to say, is the ultimate goal.

But at the river, I learned to think differently about fluency. The river has a mouth, a confluence, a flow. The river is a natural and patient form, forever making its way toward something greater than itself. Yet as the river moves, it stutters, and I do too.

Take a moment to listen to the way you talk. How do you sound? What would happen if you concentrated on the feeling of speaking? Where do you feel words in your body? Do you speak without pauses or hesitations? How often do you slip up, forget words, or have difficulty finding them in the first place? Do you sometimes shy away from speaking? Do you sometimes not want to say anything at all?

My dad took me to the river so I would feel less alone. When he pointed to the river, he gave image and language to talk about something so private and terrifying. In doing so, he connected my stuttering to the movements of the natural world and I delighted in watching my mouth move outside of itself.

Everyone who stutters does so differently. A stutter is never just a stutter but a set of intricately intimate labors with words, sound, and body. My stutter is my own and also part of a larger confluence of dysfluent mouths going about their day: ordering food at a restaurant, making small talk about the weather, or talking to loved ones. Stuttering makes me feel profoundly connected and profoundly alone. Stuttering is terrifyingly beautiful. Sometimes I want to speak without worrying; sometimes I want to speak with grace, finesse, and with all those words you can think of for smooth. But that is not me.

I talk like a river.

—J.S.

This book is for my father, Roy Scott—J.S.

To my son, Salvador—S.S.

I Talk Like a River would not have been possible without
the friendship, wisdom, and editorial brilliance of Lara LeMoal.

I would like to thank Hilary McMahon for believing in me and this story.
I would also like to thank Sydney Smith for his remarkable illustrations and
Neal Porter for his incomparable vision in bringing this work to life.

Thanks to Anuj Parikh for helping to craft the last lines,
somewhere in Guanajuato.

As always, love to my mom, Wiesia Kujawa, for giving me the gift of poetry;
and to my family, Summer, Rowan, and Sacha, for giving me the gift to go on.

—J.S.

Neal Porter Books

Text copyright © 2020 by Jordan Scott
Illustrations copyright © 2020 by Sydney Smith
All Rights Reserved
HOLIDAY HOUSE is registered in the U.S. Patent and Trademark Office.
Printed and bound in May 2020 at Toppan Leefung, Dong Guan City, China.
The artwork for this book was created with watercolor, ink, and gouache.
Book design by Jennifer Browne
www.holidayhouse.com
First Edition
10 9 8 7 6 5 4 3 2 1

Names: Scott, Jordan, 1978- author. | Smith, Sydney, 1980— illustrator.
Title: I talk like a river / by Jordan Scott ; illustrations by Sydney Smith.
Description: First edition. | New York : Holiday House, [2020] | Audience:
Ages 6-8 | Audience: Grades 2-3 | Summary: When a child has a "bad
speech day" at school, his father gives him a new perspective on his stuttering.
Identifiers: LCCN 2019022745 | ISBN 9780823445592 (hardcover)
Subjects: CYAC: Stuttering—Fiction. | Schools—Fiction. | Fathers and
sons—Fiction.
Classification: LCC PZ7.1.S336845 Iak 2020 | DDC [E]—dc23
LC record available at https://lccn.loc.gov/2019022745